SEVEN SPOOLS OF THREAD

A KWANZAA STORY

BY **ANGELA SHELF MEDEARIS**

ILLUSTRATED BY **DANIEL MINTER**

SCHOLASTIC INC.

New York Toronto London Auckland Sydney
Mexico City New Delhi Hong Kong Buenos Aires

To my father, Howard Lee Shelf, and my mother, Angeline Shelf,
whose love taught us how to be a family. To my brother, Howard, and my sisters,
Sandra and Marcia, who strive to safeguard what we've learned.
And to my husband, Michael, my daughter, Deanna, and my granddaughter,
Anysa, who teach me about true love every day. —A.S.M.

To my son, Azari Ayindé.— D.M.

ISBN 0-439-80202-4

Text copyright © 2000 by Angela Shelf Medearis. Illustrations copyright © 2000 by Daniel Minter.
All rights reserved. Published by Scholastic Inc., 557 Broadway, New York, NY 10012,
by arrangement with Albert Whitman & Company. SCHOLASTIC and associated
logos are trademarks and/or registered trademarks of Scholastic Inc.

12 11 10 9 8 7 6 5 4 3 2 1   5 6 7 8 9 10/0

Printed in the U.S.A.   40

First Scholastic printing, October 2005

The illustrations are linoleum block prints.
The text face is Woodland ITC Medium.
The display face is FC Neuland.
The design is by Scott Piehl.

Sticks in a bundle
are unbreakable

—African Proverb

Seven Spools of Thread

WAS WRITTEN ESPECIALLY for Kwanzaa. Kwanzaa is a cultural holiday begun in America and celebrated by people of African descent all over the world. In 1966, Dr. Maulana Karenga, a college professor, created Kwanzaa (KWAN-zaah), which means "first fruits" in Swahili. He based the holiday on ancient African harvest celebrations and customs. Dr. Karenga felt that African-Americans in his community needed a special time to help them take pride in their glorious past and plan for the future.

Kwanzaa is celebrated from December 26 until January 1. It is not a religious holiday or one that honors a heroic person. Instead, it is a time when people of African descent join together to honor the heritage and traditions of their ancestors. During the Kwanzaa celebration, everyone pledges to work together to improve themselves and to make their community a better place to live. Kwanzaa is a celebration of the past, the present, and the future of people of African descent.

Dr. Karenga established special symbols for Kwanzaa, including fruits and vegetables, which stand for the harvest. During the days of Kwanzaa, seven candles—one black, three red, and three green—are lighted. They stand for the Nguzo Saba (en-GOO-zoh SAH-bah), or "seven principles." The Nguzo Saba are to be memorized, discussed, and acted upon during the seven days of Kwanzaa and throughout the year.

These are the Nguzo Saba:

UMOJA (oo-MOH-jah)

UNITY: To strive for and maintain unity
in the family, community, nation and race.

KUJICHAGULIA (koo-jee-cha-goo-LEE-ah)

SELF-DETERMINATION: To define ourselves, name ourselves,
create for ourselves and speak for ourselves instead of being defined,
named, created for and spoken for by others.

UJIMA (oo-JEE-mah)

COLLECTIVE WORK AND RESPONSIBILITY: To build and
maintain our community together and make our sister's and
brother's problems our problems and to solve them together.

UJAMAA (oo-jah-MAH-ah)

CO-OPERATIVE ECONOMICS: To build and maintain our own stores,
shops and other businesses and profit from them together.

NIA (NEE-ah)

PURPOSE: To make our collective vocation the building
and developing of our community in order to restore
our people to their traditional greatness.

KUUMBA (koo-OOM-bah)

CREATIVITY: To do always as much as we can, in the way we can,
in order to leave our community more beautiful
and beneficial than we inherited it.

IMANI (ee-MAH-nee)

FAITH: To believe with all our heart in our people, our parents,
our leaders and the righteousness and victory of our struggle.

All of the principles of the Nguzo Saba are hidden in the
story SEVEN SPOOLS OF THREAD. Can you find them?

Maulana Karenga, THE AFRICAN AMERICAN HOLIDAY OF KWANZAA: A CELEBRATION OF FAMILY,
COMMUNITY AND CULTURE (Los Angeles: University of Sankore Press, 1989).

IN A SMALL **A**FRICAN VILLAGE in the country of Ghana there lived an old man and his seven sons. After the death of his wife, the old man became both father and mother to the boys. The seven brothers were handsome young men. Their skin was as smooth and dark as the finest mahogany wood. Their limbs were as straight and strong as warriors' spears.

But they were a disappointment to their father. From morning until night, the family's small home was filled with the sound of the brothers' quarreling.

As soon as the sun brought forth a new day, the brothers began to argue. They argued all morning about how to tend the crops. They argued all afternoon about the weather.

"It is hot," said the middle son.

"No—a cool breeze is blowing!" said the second son.

They argued all evening about when to return home.

"It will be dark soon," the youngest said. "Let's finish this row and begin anew tomorrow."

"No, it's too early to stop," called the third son.

"Can't you see the sun is setting?" shouted the sixth son.

And so it would continue until the moon beamed down and the stars twinkled in the sky.

At mealtime, the young men argued until the stew was cold and the fu fu was hard.

"You gave him more than you gave me," whined the third son.

"I divided the food equally," said their father.

"I will starve with only this small portion on my plate," complained the youngest.

"If you don't want it, I'll eat it!" said the oldest son. He grabbed a handful of meat from his brother's plate.

"Stop being so greedy!" said the youngest.

And so it went on every night. It was often morning before the seven brothers finished dinner.

One sad day, the old man died and was buried. At sunrise the next morning, the village Chief called the brothers before him.

"Your father has left an inheritance," said the Chief.

The brothers whispered excitedly among themselves.

"I know my father left me everything because I am the oldest son," said the oldest.

"I know my father left me everything because I am the youngest son," said the youngest.

"He left everything to me," said the middle son. "I know I was his favorite."

"Eeeh!" said the second son. "Everything is mine!"

The brothers began shouting and shoving. Soon, all seven were rolling around on the ground, hitting and kicking each other.

"Stop that this instant!" the Chief shouted.

The brothers stopped fighting. They shook the dust off their clothes and sat before the Chief, eyeing each other suspiciously.

"Your father has decreed that all of his property and possessions will be divided among you equally," said the Chief. "But first, by the time the moon rises tonight, you must learn how to make gold out of these spools of silk thread. If you do not, you will be turned out of your home as beggars."

The oldest brother received blue thread. The next brother, red. The next, yellow. The middle son was given orange thread; the next, green; the next, black; and the youngest son received white thread. For once, the brothers were speechless.

The Chief spoke again. "From this moment forward, you must not argue among yourselves or raise your hands in anger towards one another. If you do, your father's property and all his possessions will be divided equally among the poorest of the villagers. Go quickly; you only have a little time."

The brothers bowed to the Chief and hurried away.

When the seven Ashanti brothers arrived at their farm, something unusual happened. They sat side by side, from the oldest to the youngest, without saying anything unkind to each other.

"My brothers," the oldest said after a while, "let us shake hands and make peace among ourselves."

"Let us never argue or fight again," said the youngest brother.

The brothers placed their hands together and held each other tightly. For the first time in years, peace rested within the walls of their home.

"My brothers," said the third son quietly, "surely our father would not turn us into the world as beggars."

"I agree," said the middle son. "I do not believe our father would have given us the task of turning thread into gold if it were impossible."

"Could it be," said the oldest son, "that there might be small pieces of gold in this thread?"

The sun beamed hotly overhead. Yellow streams of light crept inside the hut. Each brother held up his spool of thread. The beautiful colors sparkled in the sunlight. But there were no nuggets of gold in these spools.

"I'm afraid not, my brother," said the sixth son. "But that was a good idea."

"Thank you, my brother," said the oldest.

"Could it be," said the youngest, "that by making something from this thread we could earn a fortune in gold?"

"Perhaps," said the oldest, "we could make cloth out of this thread and sell it. I believe we can do it."

"This is a good plan," said the middle son. "But we do not have enough of any one color to make a full bolt of cloth."

"What if," said the third son, "we weave the thread together to make a cloth of many colors?"

"But our people do not wear cloth like that," said the fifth son. "We wear only cloth of one color."

"Maybe," said the second, "we could make a cloth that is so special, everyone will want to wear it."

"My brothers," said the sixth son, "we could finish faster if we all worked together."

"I know we can succeed," said the middle son.

The seven Ashanti brothers went to work. Together they cut the wood to make a loom. The younger brothers held the pieces together while the older brothers assembled the loom.

They took turns weaving cloth out of their spools of thread. They made a pattern of stripes and shapes that looked like the wings of birds. They used all the colors— blue, red, yellow, orange, green, black, and white. Soon the brothers had several pieces of beautiful multicolored cloth.

When the cloth was finished, the seven brothers took turns neatly folding the brightly colored fabric. Then they placed it into seven baskets and put the baskets on their heads.

The brothers formed a line from the oldest to the youngest and began the journey to the village. The sun slowly made a golden path across the sky. The brothers hurried down the long, dusty road as quickly as they could.

As soon as they entered the marketplace, the seven Ashanti brothers called out, "Come and buy the most wonderful cloth in the world! Come and buy the most wonderful cloth in the world!"

They unfolded a bolt and held it up for all to see. The multicolored fabric glistened like a rainbow. A crowd gathered around the seven Ashanti brothers.

"Oh," said one villager. "I have never seen cloth so beautiful! Look at the unusual pattern!"

"Ah," said another. "This is the finest fabric in all the land! Feel the texture!"

The brothers smiled proudly. Suddenly, a man dressed in magnificent robes pushed his way to the front of the crowd. Everyone stepped back respectfully. It was the King's treasurer. He rubbed the cloth between the palms of his hands. Then he held it up to the sunlight.

"What a thing of beauty," he said, fingering the material. "This cloth will make a wonderful gift for the King! I must have all of it."

The seven brothers whispered together.

"Cloth fit for a king," said the oldest, "should be purchased at a price only a king can pay. It is yours for one bag of gold."

"Sold," said the King's treasurer. He untied his bag of gold and spilled out many pieces for the brothers.

The seven Ashanti brothers ran out of the market-place and back down the road to their village.

A shining silver moon began to creep up in the sky. Panting and dripping with sweat, the brothers threw themselves before the Chief's hut.

"Oh, Chief," said the oldest, "we have turned the thread into gold!"

The Chief came out of his hut and sat upon a stool.

The oldest brother poured the gold out onto the ground.

"Have you argued or fought today?" asked the Chief.

"No, my Chief," said the youngest. "We have been too busy working together to argue or fight."

"Then you have learned the lesson your father sought to teach you," said the Chief. "All that he had is now yours."

The older brothers smiled happily, but the youngest son looked sad.

"What about the poor people in the village?" he asked. "We receive an inheritance, but what will they do?"

"Perhaps," said the oldest, "we can teach them how to turn thread into gold."

The Chief smiled. "You have learned your lesson very well."

The seven Ashanti brothers taught their people carefully. The village became famous for its beautiful, multicolored cloth, and the villagers prospered.

From that day until this, the seven Ashanti brothers have worked together, farming the land.

And they have worked peacefully, in honor of their father.

WEAVING CLOTH – AFRICAN STYLE

The people of Ghana, West Africa, are famous for their woven cloth. The patterns vary from tribe to tribe. Kente, which is made of silken threads in a rainbow of colors, is one type of cloth that is woven in Ghana.

In Ghana, men usually use small, portable looms that they can carry from village to village. They trade the 4-to-6 inch strips of woven cloth for food and other supplies. Larger pieces of cloth are usually crafted by women. They use heavy looms capable of turning out squares of fabric about 16 x 20 inches wide. After the cloth has been woven, the strips are sewn together to make clothing, carpets, or blankets.

You can make a simple loom to weave a strip of cloth that can be worn as a belt.

THINGS YOU WILL NEED
4 plastic straws
1 skein 4-ply worsted yarn
scissors

WEAVING CLOTH TO MAKE A BELT

1.

Cut four pieces of yarn, each 80 inches long.

2.

Then cut 1/2 inch off the end of each straw.
Keep the 1/2-inch pieces. They will be used later.

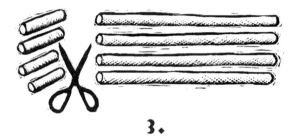

3.

Slide one of the shortened straws almost to the end
of one of the pieces of yarn. Sucking on one end of the straw
will help to draw the yarn through quickly.

4.

Loop the yarn and pull the other end through the straw. Place a finger
in the loop to prevent the yarn from pulling all the way through the straw.
Pull the loose ends of the yarn until they are even.
Leave a 1/2-inch loop of yarn at one end of the straw.

5.

Tie the loop into a loose knot. Slip a 1/2-inch piece of straw into the knot. The straw should look like a T on the end. This will prevent the thread from slipping through the straw during the weaving process. Repeat steps 2 through 5 to thread the remaining straws.

6.

Tie the end of the wool on the skein to the top straw. Tightly weave the yarn in and out between the straws. When your weave is 3-to-4 inches long, push it off the straw towards the loosely knotted end.

7.

Continue weaving until the woven part of the belt is the length you desire. Tie the loose yarn into a tight knot. Let the long ends hang down about 8 inches to make a fringe. Cut off any excess yarn. Now your belt is ready to wear or to give as a gift during Kwanzaa.

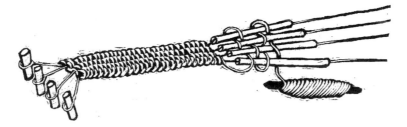